POKéMON
THE JOHTO JOURNEYS
POP QUIZ #2

by Tracey West

SCHOLASTIC INC.
New York Toronto London Auckland Sydney
Mexico City New Delhi Hong Kong Buenos Aires

ISBN 0-439-41292-7



12 11 10 9 8 7 6 5 4 3 2 1     2 3 4 5 6 7/0

Cover Design by Bethany Dixon
Book Design by Keirsten Geise and Bethany Dixon

Printed in the U.S.A.
First Scholastic printing, May 2002

# Table of Contents

***So you wanna be a master of Pokémon? Do you have the skills to be number one?***

## Introduction

Greetings! I am Professor Oak of Pallet Town. If you are reading this book, then you must be a Pokémon Trainer on the road to becoming a Pokémon Master.

As I always tell my young friend Ash Ketchum, it takes hard work and dedication to become a Pokémon Master. Besides collecting, training, and battling your Pokémon, it's important to know about all of the Pokémon in the Pokémon universe.

That is why I have put together this book of Pokémon quizzes. Inside you'll find questions about **Pokémon** and the **Pokémon cartoon episodes**, as well as **visual puzzlers**, **matching activities**, and other **brain teasers**. This book is filled with questions about the **original 150 Pokémon** and the **100 new Pokémon** that can be found in the Johto Region. You'll need to keep up with all of the changes in the Pokémon world to master this book.

After you tackle the quizzes, look in the back of the book to see if your answers were correct. Then add up the number of correct answers to find out what it takes to really become a Pokémon Master.

That's enough from me for now. I don't want to keep you from your challenge.

Good luck!

# Who's My Trainer?

Each group of Pokémon has the same trainer. Name the character from the Pokémon cartoon that trains all three. Write the trainer's name in the spaces below. Is it Jessie, Misty, Ash, Brock, or James? You decide!

_______________ 1. Bayleef™ Noctowl™ Cyndaquil™

_______________ 2. Crobat™ Pineco™ Geodude™

_______________ 3. Wobbuffet™ Arbok™

_______________ 4. Poliwhirl™ Starmie™ Togepi™

# Episode Expert I

How well do you know the Pokémon cartoon show? To find out, tackle these questions based on Ash's adventures in the Johto Region. If you need to brush up first, tune into the Kids WB! network to catch your favorite episodes. Circle the correct answer to each question.

1. Which three Pokémon do new trainers in the Johto Region get to choose from?

A. Sunflora, Politoed, and Magby

B. Chikorita, Totodile, and Cyndaquil

C. Bulbasaur, Squirtle, and Charmander

2. What is Heracross's favorite snack?

A. rice balls

B. bananas

C. tree sap and nectar

3. How did Spinarak help Officer Jenny catch criminals?

A. by spinning a sticky web to trap them

B. by stunning them with poison darts

C. by hypnotizing them

4. Who did Ash's Chikorita have a little crush on?

A. Ash

B. Brock

C. Pikachu

5. Why did Ash need a Hoothoot to travel through the Dark Forest?

A. to help stop attacks from Grass Pokémon

B. so he could fly above the trees

C. to see through ghostly illusions

6. What happens to Mareep when they make contact with electricity?

A. they run away

B. their fleece puffs up

C. they can fly

7. Who won the Pokémon Fire-and-Rescue Grand Prix?

A. the Golduck team

B. the Squirtle Squad

C. the Super Squad

8. What unhappy little Pokémon tried to disguise itself as a Hoppip?

A. Oddish

B. Charizard

C. Pichu

9. The sound of what instrument kept Alicia's Wooper in line?

A. drums

B. bugle

C. tambourine

10. What valuable items were Rochelle's Donphan able to find?

A. Poké Balls

B. Berries

C. Amberite

**Poké Note**

Heracross was the very first Pokémon Ash captured when he reached the Johto Region.

# Pokémon: Up Close and Personal I

Look at these close-up photos of Pokémon. Can you name that Pokémon?

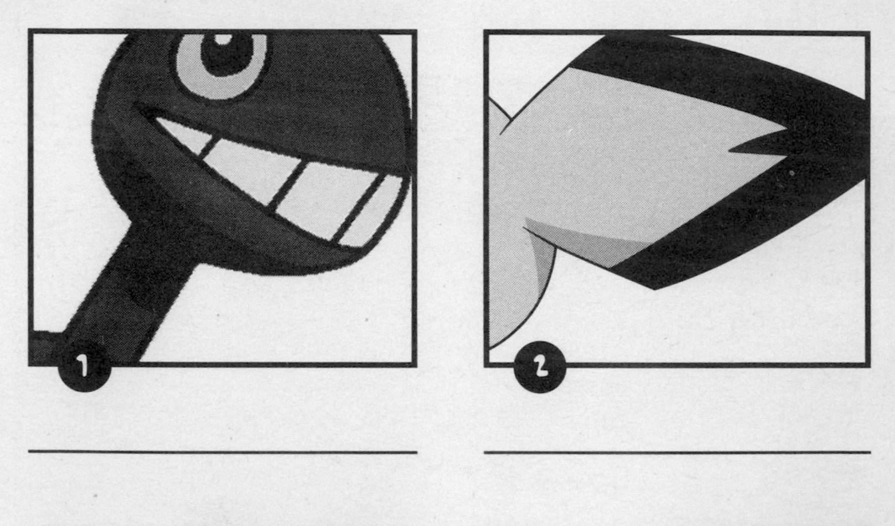

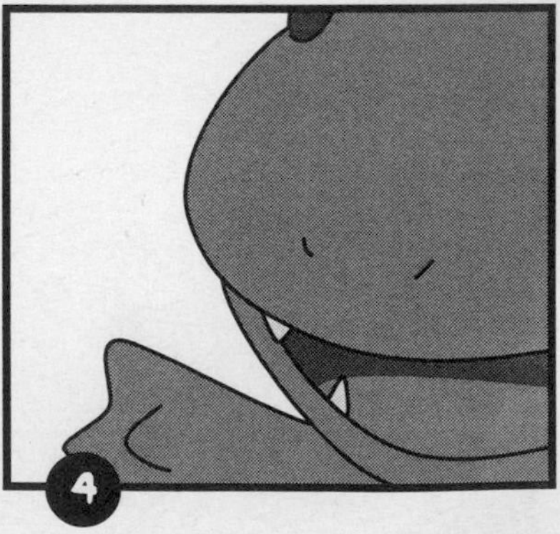

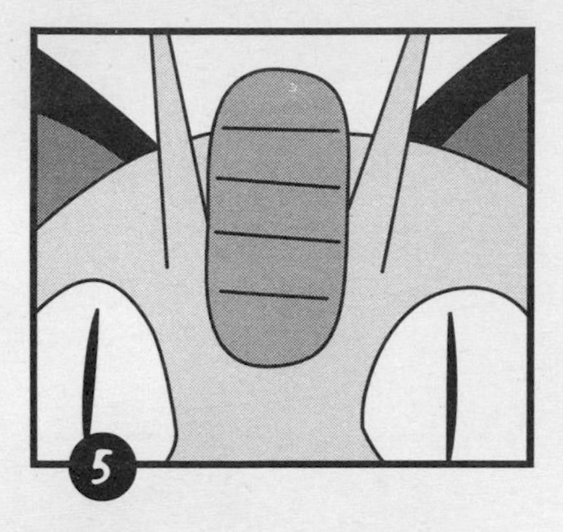
5

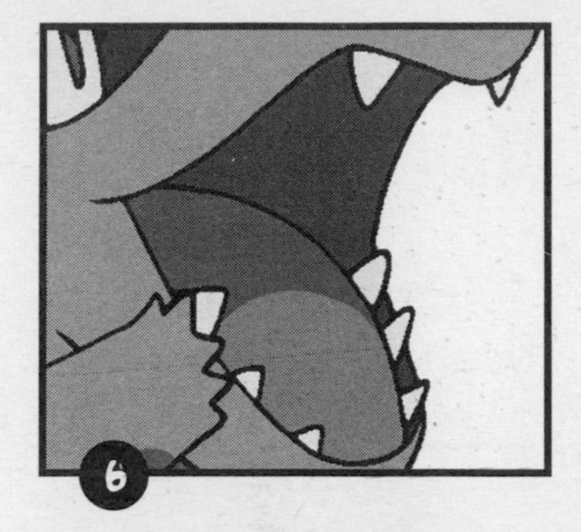
6

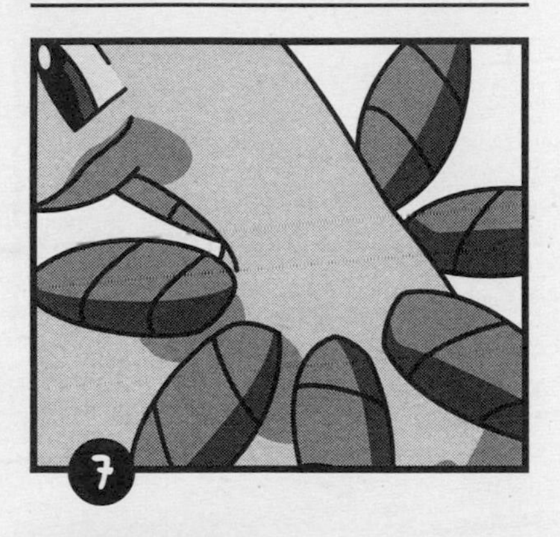
7

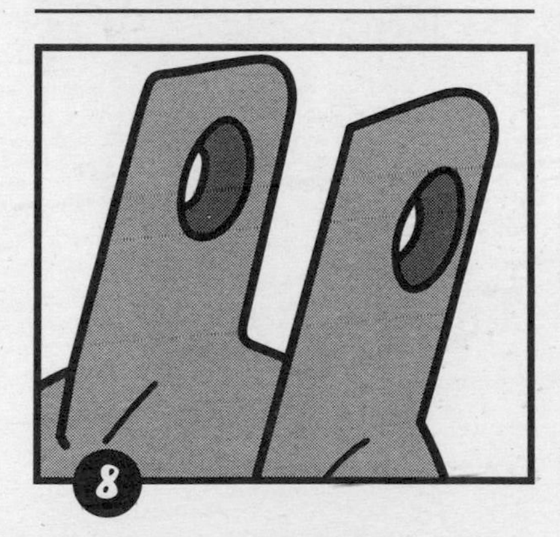
8

9

10

# Name That Pokémon I

Which Pokémon . . .

1. . . . has spicy-smelling leaves that grow out of its neck? ______________________

2. . . . loves honey and has a crescent-shaped mark on its forehead? ______________________

3. . . . has a powerful tail which looks like a hand? ______________________

4. is so light that it gets picked up into the air when a breeze blows? ______________________

5. comes out at night and stands on one foot at a time? ______________________

6. . . . produces delicious, nutritious milk? ______

7. . . . carries passengers on its back across large bodies of water? ______________________

8. . . . exhibits odd powers if it gets a terrible headache? ______________________

9. . . . launches kicks while spinning around on its head? ______________________

10. . . . makes nests on top of high cliffs and is known for making deliveries? ____________

11. . . . closes its petals when the sun goes down and doesn't open them again until sunrise? ____________

12. . . . shoots flame out of its back when it is attacked or surprised? ____________

13. . . . has two sets of wings and a powerful Supersonic Attack? ____________

14. . . . spins a web and has markings on its back that look like a face? ____________

15. . . . is cute, but feels slimy and slippery when you try to catch it? ____________

16. . . . is the evolution of Eevee known as the Moonlight Pokémon? ____________

17. . . . has 26 different shapes that resemble an alphabet? ____________

18. . . . uses the round balls on its antlers to hypnotize others? ____________

19. . . . weighs over 1,000 pounds and loves to eat and sleep? ____________

20. . . . makes a pretty sound when it does its Petal Dance? ____________

# Poké Match I

Match the Pokémon on this page to its type on the next page. Draw a line connecting the correct pairing.

1. Hitmontop™
2. Noctowl™
3. Wobbuffet™
4. Hoppip™
5. Magby™
6. Houndour™
7. Scizor™
8. Croconaw™
9. Pineco™
10. Ledyba™
11. Sentret™
12. Pichu™
13. Smoochum™
14. Phanpy™
15. Sudowoodo™

A. Fire

B. Water

C. Normal

D. Dark/Fire

E. Ice/Psychic

F. Grass/Flying

G. Ground

H. Fighting

I. Rock

J. Dark/Flying

K. Bug

L. Bug/Steel

M. Bug/Flying

N. Psychic

O. Electric

## Poké Note

In the Johto Region, Ash discovered two new types of Pokémon: Steel and Dark. Murkrow is one example of this new type — it's a Dark/Flying Pokémon that is believed to bring misfortune to all who come in contact with it.

# Pokémon Stadium I

In the following battles, decide which Pokémon is likely to win, based on their Types. Assume that all the Pokémon have the same amount of energy and experience. Then circle the Pokémon you think would come out on top!

**Poké Note**

If a friendly trainer asks you to battle your Pokémon, you should always agree. It's rude to refuse!

1. Totodile™ vs. Cyndaquil™

2. Golem™ vs. Mareep™

3. Chikorita™ vs. Magby™

4. Pichu™ vs. Politoed™

5. Phanpy™ vs. Hoothoot™

6. Smoochum™ vs. Misdreavus™

# Evolution Mix-up

Which one is not like the others? In each of the following groups, one Pokémon does not fit. Decide which Pokémon is not part of the chain of evolution.

1. Totodile™ → Croconaw™ → Gyarados™

2. Oddish™ → Chinchou™ → Lanturn™

3. Elekid™ → Pikachu™ → Raichu™

4. Ledyba™ → Ledian™ → Ariados™

5. Skiploom™ → Gloom™ → Bellossom™

6. Cyndaquil™ → Charmeleon™ → Typhlosion™

  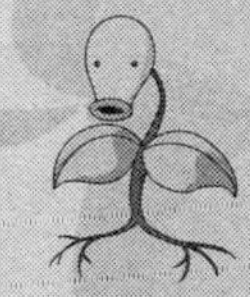

7. Sunkern™ → Sunflora™ → Bellsprout™

  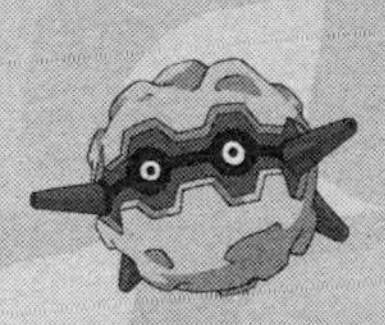

8. Pineco™ → Cloyster™ → Forretress™

9. Hoothoot™ → Delibird™ → Noctowl™

10. Smoochum™ → Jynx™ → Hitmonchan™

# Poké Math

Ready for some Poké-rithmetic? Use the blank spaces to fill in your answer. (Hint: sometimes part of an answer might be zero.)

1. What is the number of heads on Weezing *plus* the number of leaves on Chikorita's head?

_______ + _______ = _______

2. What is the number of legs a Ledyba has *minus* the number of tails a Tauros has?

_______ – _______ = _______

3. What is the number of wings on Crobat *plus* the number of prongs on top of Elekid's head?

_______ + _______ = _______

4. What is the number of arms that Pikachu has *minus* the number of arms Wooper has?

_______ – _______ = _______

5. What is the number of heads on Dodrio *plus* the number of eggs in Blissey's pouch?

_______ + _______ = _______

6. What is the number of legs a Bayleef has *minus* the number of legs Gengar has?

_______ – _______ = _______

7. What is the number of jewels in Espeon's forehead *plus* the number of tails a Koffing has?

_______ + _______ = _______

8. What is the number of Magnemite it takes to make one Magneton *minus* the total number of evolutions in the Totodile family?

_______ – _______ = _______

9. What is the number of lightning bolts on Elekid's chest *plus* the number of circles on Urasaring's chest? _______ + _______ = _______

10. What is the number of flowers on Bellossom's head *minus* the number of flowers on Skiploom's head? _______ – _______ = _______

11. What is the number of faces that make one Exeggute *plus* the number of arms Slugma has?

_______ + _______ = _______

12. What is the number of different types of Unown *minus* the number of legs a Spinarak has? _______ – _______ = _______

# Poké Puzzle

Ash often has to solve some mysteries while traveling through the Johto Region. What kind of Pokémon detective are you? Use the clues below to fill in the crossword puzzle on page 23.

1. The color of a Bayleef.

2. Ash's first Pokémon.

4. This soft stuff covers the body of Pokémon like Growlithe and Furret.

6. The answer to the question: Does Ash wear a blue baseball cap?

7. Ash met four sisters who trained this Pokémon.

8. This little pink Pokémon is shaped like a star.

9. After you catch a Pokémon, you should ______________ it.

10. The direction a Hoppip will fall if the wind stops blowing.

11. This Dark Pokémon is the last evolutionary form of Eevee.

14. ________ Ketchum of Pallet Town.

17. What Jigglypuff likes to do best.

18. Ash and this legendary Pokémon starred in the movie *Pokémon 2000: The Power of One*.

19. Caterpie and Ledyba are both ________ Pokémon.

20. Ash's orange-haired friend.

## Down

1. Team Rocket's boss

2. This man gives trainers their start in the Johto Region.

3. This Grass/Flying Pokémon evolves into Skiploom.

4. Ash won a ZephyrBadge by beating this Violet City gym leader.

5. It's known as the Littlebear Pokémon.

6. This small bird Pokémon evolves into Xatu.

7. In order for Pichu to become Pikachu, it must ______________.

12. This Fire Pokémon evolves into Magmar.

13. Smoochum has an attack called Sweet ____________.

15. This word describes the size of a Snorlax.

16. Doduo can't fly, but it can __Run__ very fast.

# Poké Match II

Match each Pokémon to its evolved form. Draw a line connecting the correct pairing.

# Poké Match III

Match the character on the Pokémon TV show, *The Johto Journeys*, to his or her description.

1. Kurt
2. Arielle
3. Casey
4. Liza
5. Gligarman

A. Trains Ledyba using a whistle.

B. Runs the Charizard preserve where Ash's Charizard decided to stay so it could learn to become a better Pokémon.

C. Is a Poké Ball expert who makes Poké Balls out of Apricorn and likes to dress up like Slowpoke.

D. Fights crime dressed as a certain Ground/ Flying Pokémon and asked Ash to take over the job of superhero.

E. Trains a Chikorita that evolved into Bayleef and is crazy about baseball.

# Name that Type

Name the type that each group of Pokémon has in common. Write your answer in the space provided. The first one has been done for you.

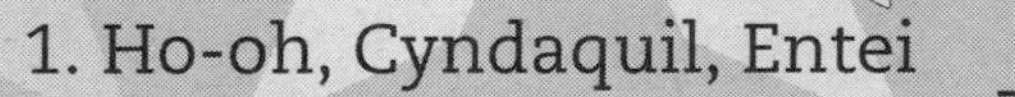

1. Ho-oh, Cyndaquil, Entei Fire

2. Squirtle, Azumarill, Kabutops ____________

3. Drowzee, Mewtwo, Unown ____________

4. Hitmonlee, Hitmontop, Tyrogue ____________

5. Meowth, Stantler, Togetic ____________________

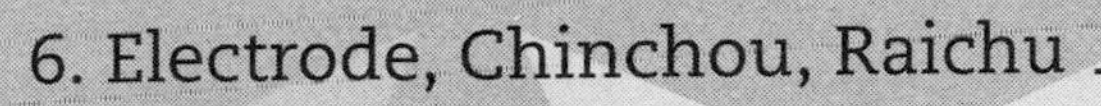

6. Electrode, Chinchou, Raichu ____________________

7. Chikorita, Sunflora, Jumpluff ____________________

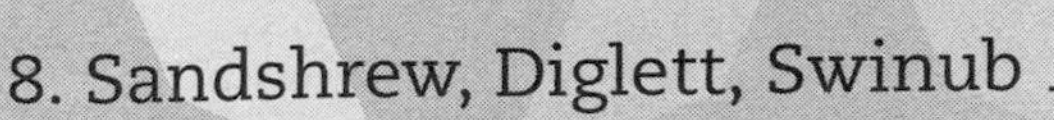

8. Sandshrew, Diglett, Swinub ____________________

# Name That Pokémon II

Circle the correct answer to each question.

1. Which of these Water Pokémon has super strong jaws that can crush almost anything?

   A. Lanturn

   B. Azumarill

   C. Totodile

2. Which of these Pokémon did Brock agree to take care of for his friend Suzie?

   A. Vulpix

   B. Geodude

   C. Onix

3. Which of these Ghost Pokémon walks on two legs?

   A. Gastly

   B. Gengar

   C. Haunter

4. Which of these Ground Pokémon is blue and has a trunk?

A. Sandshrew

B. Phanpy

C. Marowak

5. Which one of these Pokémon can new trainers get from Professor Oak?

A. Chikorita

B. Charmander

C. Charizard

6. Which of these Pokémon would Misty most likely be afraid of?

A. Tentacruel

B. Chinchou

C. Ariados

7. Which one of these Pokémon does not have a tail?

A. Poliwag

B. Poliwhirl

C. Croconaw

8. Which one of these Pokémon is capable of evolving?

A. Jigglypuff

B. Lugia

C. Aipom

9. Which one of these Pokémon is too hot to touch?

A. Magby

B. Skiploom

C. Meowth

10. Which one of these Pokémon is no bigger than a foot tall?

A. Snorlax

B. Steelix

C. Togepi

**Poké Note**

Jessie of Team Rocket may not be happy with her Wobbuffet, but in the Johto Region, there is an entire town that loves these strange Pokémon.

# Color Quiz

Two of the Pokémon in each row are the same color. Circle the Pokémon that does not match the other two.

1. Igglybuff™ → Teddiursa™ → Blissey™

2. Pikachu™ → Elekid™ → Flaaffy™

3. Larvitar™ → Slugma™ → Magby™

4. Houndoom™ → Marill™ → Umbreon™

5. Sentret™ → Stantler™ → Porygon 2™

6. Diglett™ → Meganium™ → Weedle™

7. Raichu™ → Horsea™ → Quagsire™

  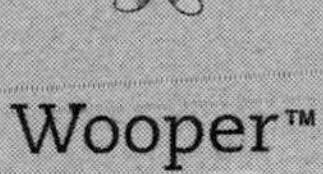

8. Chinchou™ → Wooper™ → Corsola™

9. Lickitung™ → Crobat™ → Hoppip™

10. Chikorita™ → Caterpie™ → Smoochum™

# Pokémon A–Z

Did you know that there is a Pokémon for each letter of the alphabet? Use the clues to figure out which Pokémon is being described in this alphabetical quiz.

1. This Pokémon is part of the legendary bird trio with Moltres and Zapdos: A__________

2. This one of Ash's Pokémon refused to evolve into Ivysaur: B__________

3. This Water/Rock Pokémon is known as the Coral Pokémon: C__________

4. This Ground Pokémon has strong tusks and a powerful Roll Out Attack: D__________

5. This evolved form of Eevee has Psychic powers: E__________

6. This Water Pokémon has really powerful jaws: F__________

7. This super slimy Pokémon evolves into Muk: G__________

8. This Pokémon hypnotizes its opponents with sleep waves: H______________________

9. It's cute! It's round! It's pink! It evolves into Jigglypuff! It's J______________________!

10. This Pokémon's opponents get a real jolt out of its lightning-charged electric attacks: J______________________

11. The third and final evolution of Horsea and Seadra is K______________________

12. This legendary Pokémon rules the seas: L______________________

13. James of Team Rocket once spent a lot of money buying this common, orange Water Pokémon: M______________________

14. Ash trains one of these Pokémon, which has excellent eyesight at night: N______________________

15. This Water Pokémon traps its enemies with its suction-cupped tentacles: O______________________

16. Poliwhirl can evolve into Poliwrath, or this cute green Frog Pokémon: P______________________

17. This Fire Pokémon can shoot flames from its back and from the top of its head: Q________________________________

18. You can find this Pokémon clinging to the bottom of Mantine, scavenging for food: R________________________________

19. This odd Pokémon can paint using the tip of its tail: S__________________________

20. Both this Pokémon and Togepi like to spread happiness, and have triangle designs on their bodies: T____________________

21. It's big! It's brown! And it can snap a tree in half with its bare hands. It's U______________!

22. Poor James! This Pokémon loves to swallow him up: V__________________________

23. Poor Jessie! This Pokémon is always popping up when she least expects it: W______________

24. This combination Psychic/Flying Pokémon is the evolved form of Natu: X________________

25. This combination Bug/Flying Pokémon once stole Ash's hat: Y ____________________

26. Brock trained this Pokémon, which lives in dark places and uses a radar system to locate its enemies: 2 ____________________

## Poké Note

Ho-oh just might be the most colorful Pokémon of all. A legend says that its body glows in seven colors, and a rainbow forms behind it when it flies!

## Poké Note

For Fighting Pokémon Tyrogue, evolution is three times the fun. It can evolve into either Hitmontop, Hitmonlee, or Hitmonchan!

# Episode Expert II

So you think you're an episode expert? Try answering this next batch of questions about the Pokémon cartoon.

1. What shape objects do Quagsire like best?

    A. square objects

    B. diamond-shaped objects

    C. round objects

2. What happened to the Sunflora when Team Rocket gave them a super dose of sunlight?

    A. They shrank.

    B. Their heads grew huge.

    C. They flew away.

3. Ash, Brock, and Misty met a Marill that wouldn't stop crying. Why was Marill so sad?

    A. It couldn't find its trainer.

    B. It couldn't win any battles.

    C. It was hungry.

4. What is special about the Noctowl that Ash caught?

   A. Its wings and tail are red.

   B. It has an extra foot.

   C. Its beak is extra large.

5. What Pokémon did Ash catch to win the Bug-Catching Contest?

   A. Scyther

   B. Ledian

   C. Beedrill

6. Who did Ash battle in order to catch Totodile?

   A. Team Rocket

   B. Misty

   C. Gary

7. Which performer in the Pokémon Circus did Totodile fall in love with?

   A. Azumarill

   B. Clefairy

   C. Corsola

8. Which event happens just before the Pokémon Swap Meet?

   A. the running of the Tauros

   B. the swimming of the Magikarp

   C. the singing of the Jigglypuff

9. Which Pokémon did Misty's Togepi get lost with?

   A. a baby Gyarados

   B. Pichu

   C. a baby Sentret

10. Why do the people of Blenn Town keep Psychic Pokémon as partners?

A. to make fortune cookies

B. to keep Ghost Pokémon away

C. to run a psychic telephone service

## Poké Note

Girafarig is a Psychic Pokémon that Ash met in Blenn Town. This Pokémon has a special attack called Future Sight that allows it to launch an attack that won't hit its opponent until a few moments into the future!

# Pokémon: Up Close and Personal II

Look at these close-up photos of Pokémon. Can you tell which Pokémon is pictured?

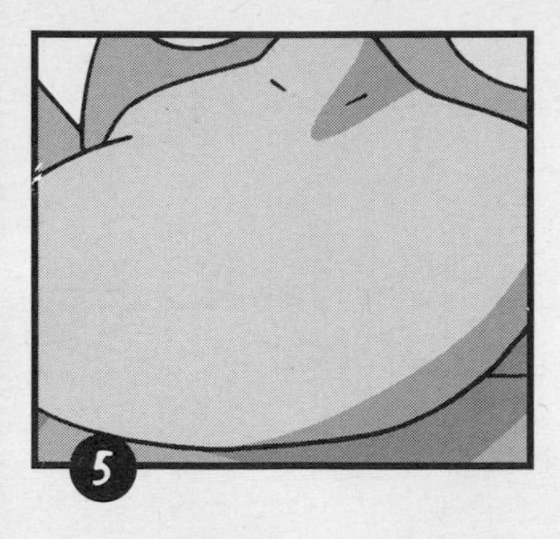
5

6

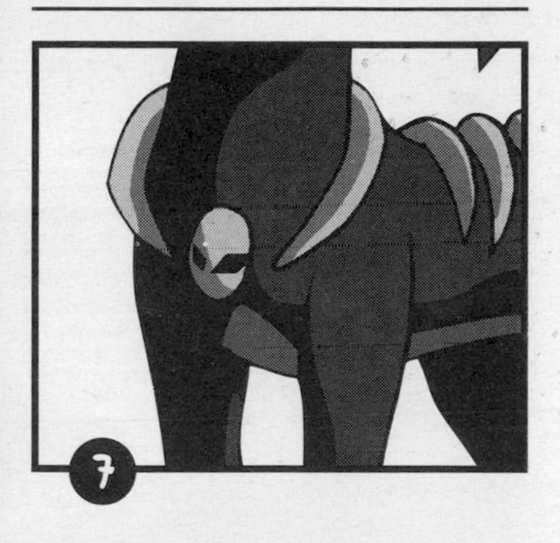
7

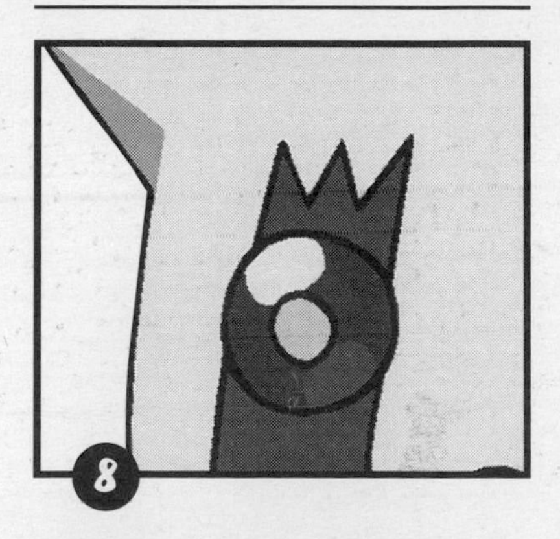
8

9

10

# Name That Human

Use the cheat sheet to fill in these sentences about some of the human characters who populate the Pokémon cartoon.

1. ________________ battled his rival Gary in Pallet Town before heading to the Johto Region.

2. __________________ is terrified of Bug Pokémon.

3. _________________________ falls in love with just about every girl he sees.

4. __________________ made friends with a Blissey in nursing school.

5. ______________ gets attacked by his Victreebell every time he calls on it.

6. ______________ rents out Hoothoot to travelers passing through her mysterious forest.

7. ____________ challenged Ash to a contest to see who could catch an unusual Noctowl.

8. ________________ is Ecruteak City gym leader who battles with Ghost Pokémon.

9. ____________________ is a Pokémon photographer who sometimes hangs out with Ash, Brock, and Misty.

10. ______________________ is a ninja who defeats Team Rocket with her Venonat.

## Cheat Sheet

Ash

Aya

Brock

James

Jessie

Hagatha

Misty

Morty

Dr. Wiseman

Todd

# True or False?

How much do you really know about Ash, Misty, Brock, and their Pokémon? See if you can answer these True/False questions about them. Circle T for True and F for False.

1. Misty's favorite Pokémon is her Psyduck. T F

2. Ash made it into the Orange League Hall of Fame. T F

3. Officer Jenny has a crush on Brock. T F

4. Ash's Pikachu loves to be inside its Poké Ball. T F

5. Brock is a good cook. T F

6. Squirtle left Ash to go off with Officer Jenny and the Squirtle Squad. T F

7. Ash's Chikorita once tried to run away. T F

8. One of Misty's Pokémon is a Krabby. T F

9. Brock was happy to leave Professor Ivy and return to Pallet Town. T F

10. Ash released his Bulbasaur back into the wild. T F

11. Brock caught a Heracross in the Johto Region. T F

12. Ash's gym badges were once stolen by some Murkrow. T F

13. Team Rocket has never managed to steal Pikachu. T F

14. Brock's Zubat has never evolved. T F

15. Misty's Togepi doesn't know any attacks. T F

16. After Brock saved Stantler from Team Rocket, he caught it in a Poké Ball. T F

17. One of Ash's Pokémon is Tauros. T F

18. Brock comes from Cerulean City. T F

19. Geodude has sharp teeth. T F

20. Cyndaquil can use Poison Attacks. T F

21. Poliwhirl is the final Evolved form of Poliwag. T F

22. Pineco can use a Self-Destruct Attack. T F

23. Togepi once became friends with a Houndoom. T F

24. Noctowl can evolve into Hoothoot. T F

25. Starmie can use a Tackle Attack. T F

# Pokémon Super Scramble

There are at least 100 new kinds of Pokémon to discover in the Johto Region! Use the clues to see if you can unscramble the names of these Johto Pokémon:

1. Known as the Scout Pokémon, it is always on the lookout for danger.
   **T N E E T S R** ____________________

2. Ash caught one of these small Grass Pokémon in the Johto Region.
   **O K R T A I C H I** ____________________

3. This Bug/Flying Pokémon is red with black spots on its back.
   **B A D E L Y** ____________________

4. This cute Pokémon evolves into Clefairy.
   **F L E C A F** ______________________

5. This combination Water/Electric Pokémon communicates by means of constantly flashing lights.
   **H O U N I C H C** ______________________

6. The seed Pokémon evolves into Sunflora.
   **R E N S K U N** ______________________

7. This Pokémon might be called a Fairy Pokémon, but it looks super tough with its massive fangs.
   **R U N G B A L L** ______________________

8. This legendary Pokémon is said to have the magical ability to purify polluted water.
   **N I C E S U U** ______________________

9. This Pokémon lives in the sea but enjoys flying out of the water and over the waves.
   **T E A M I N N** ______________________

10. The body of this winged Pokémon is covered with steel armor.
    **M O A R R S K Y** ______________________

# Poké Match IV

Every Pokémon Master knows that different Pokémon can be found in different places. Match each Pokémon on this page to the place you are most likely to find it.

1. Lanturn
2. Magcargo
3. Electabuzz
4. Mr. Mime
5. Gligar
6. Golduck
7. Skarmory
8. Zubat
9. Pineco
10. Larvitar
11. Blissey
12. Sneasel

A. hanging from the side of a cliff

B. hanging from a tree

C. in a dark cave

D. nesting in a bramble bush

E. deep in the ocean

F. deep underground

G. at a power plant

H. helping Ash's mom

I. raiding a Pidgey nest

J. by a volcano

K. swimming along a lake

L. helping Nurse Joy at a Pokémon Center

# Name That Pokémon III

One of the most challenging things about being a Pokémon Master is keeping track of the Pokémon's strange names. If you know the difference between Bellossom and Bellsprout, then you should be able to ace this quiz. Circle the correct answer.

1. Which of these Pokémon can't fly?

   A. Hoppip

   B. Houndour

   C. Ho-oh

2. Which of these Pokémon is the tallest?

   A. Totodile

   B. Togetic

   C. Tyranitar

3. Which of these Pokémon is pink and often kept as a pet?

   A. Snubbull

   B. Smeargle

   C. Shuckle

4. Which of these Pokémon can use a Water Gun Attack?

   A. Croconaw

   B. Crobat

   C. Cubone

5. Which of these Pokémon stores electricity in its furry fleece?

   A. Cleffa

   B. Flaaffy

   C. Jumpluff

6. Which of these Pokémon can poison you with its toxic spikes?

   A. Quilava

   B. Qwilfish

   C. Quagsire

7. Which of these Pokémon causes volcanoes to erupt when it barks?

   A. Entei

   B. Espeon

   C. Eevee

8. Which of these Pokémon absorbs sunlight with its petals?

   A. Skiploom

   B. Spinarak

   C. Skarmory

9. Which of these Pokémon has rings on its body that glow when darkness falls?

A. Umbreon

B. Ursaring

C. Unown

10. Which of these Pokémon is known as "the kicking Pokémon"?

A. Hitmontop

B. Hitmonlee

C. Hitmonchan

# Pokémon Stadium II

Ready for another stadium challenge? Based on Type, decide which Pokémon would win the following battles. Assume that each Pokémon has the same amount of experience.

1. Yanma™ vs. Tangela™

2. Nidorino™ vs. Donphan™

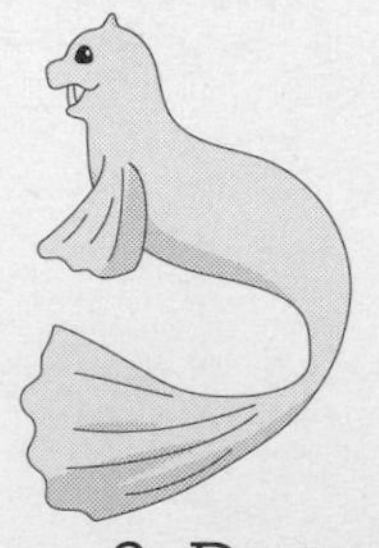

3. Dewgong™ vs. Tyrogue™

4. Delibird™ vs. Octillery™

5. Scyther™ vs. Mr. Mime™

6. Ledian™ vs. Quilava™

7. Pidgey™ vs. Elekid™

8. Croconaw™ vs. Sandshrew™

# Team Rocket Trivia

Use the cheat sheet on this page to fill in the following facts about those infamous would-be Pokémon thieves, Team Rocket.

## Cheat Sheet

Arbotank
bottle caps
Butch
Cassidy
language
Lickitung
mask
Meowth
money
net
nurse
Poison
robot
Shuckle
Sunflora
Wobbuffet

1. James loves to collect colorful ______________.

2. ____________________ and ____________________ are Team Rocket's rivals.

3. Jessie studied to be a ______________ before joining Team Rocket.

4. Meowth is jealous of ________________ for stealing its line in the Team Rocket motto.

5. Meowth has tried to win two Pokémon contests by disguising itself as a ________________.

6. Pokémon became attracted to Team Rocket after they drank purple ________________ juice.

7. Team Rocket made a mechanical desert tank and called it ______________________________.

8. Jessie accidentally traded her Pokémon ________________ at the Pokémon Swap Meet.

9. Jessie, James, and Meowth never seem to have enough ________________________.

10. Team Rocket once disguised themselves as a ventriloquist trio and pretended that ______________________ was a dummy.

11. Jessie once gained special powers over Pokémon when she put on an ancient ____________________________.

12. James's Weezing is a ____________________ Pokémon.

13. Team Rocket used a ____________________
to capture a flock of Mareep.

14. Meowth can translate the ________________
of other Pokémon.

15. Team Rocket used a giant ________________
to try and capture wild Stantler.

# Episode Expert III

Okay, hotshots! Here's your final chance to prove that you know it all when it comes to the Pokémon TV cartoon. Circle the correct answer to each question.

1. What does Old Man Shuckle do with the Shuckle juice he makes?

   A. He turns it into soda pop.

   B. He makes a special healing medicine.

   C. He drinks it for breakfast.

2. What happened at the Grass Pokémon tournament?

   A. New trainer Efram beat Ash with his Skiploom.

   B. Ash beat Efram using Bulbasaur.

   C. Team Rocket won by cheating.

3. Which Pokémon led Ash to victory when he battled Ghost Pokémon to win the Fog Badge?

A. Pikachu

B. Bulbasaur

C. Noctowl

4. What kind of Poké Ball did Brock use to catch his Pineco?

A. a Pine Ball

B. a Fast Ball

C. a Bug Ball

5. How did Ash and his friends travel safely through the Onix Tunnel?

A. Jigglypuff put the Onix to sleep.

B. Brock tamed all of the Onix

C. Team Rocket stole all of the Onix.

6. In one episode, Misty got stuck with James while Meowth and Jessie got stuck with Ash and Brock. How did this happen?

   A. Psyduck's Confusion Attack got them mixed up.

   B. They were attacked by a forest full of angry Ursaring.

   C. Misty and Jessie decided to switch places.

7. What badge did Ash win after battling Bugsy in the Azalea Town gym?

   A. a Red Badge

   B. a Bug Badge

   C. a Hive Badge

8. Which Pokémon attacked the sick Houndour that Ash tried to help?

   A. Golem

   B. Gengar

   C. Onix

9. Who did Ash beat to win a Plain Badge?

A. Jessie and Wobbuffet

B. Whitney and Miltank

C. Liza and Charla

10. Which Pokémon were guilty of gobbling up all the apples in an orchard?

A. Totodile

B. Pichu

C. Dunsparce

**Poké Note**

Ursaring have a special talent — they can find food buried underground. If only Team Rocket could be so lucky!

# Answers

## WHO'S MY TRAINER?

(page 3)

1. Ash
2. Brock
3. Jessie
4. Misty

## EPISODE EXPERT I

(pages 4-7)

1. B
2. C
3. A
4. A
5. C
6. B
7. B
8. A
9. C
10. C

## POKÉMON: UP CLOSE AND PERSONAL I

(pages 8-9)

1. Girafarig
2. Pichu
3. Chinchou
4. Charmander
5. Meowth
6. Totodile
7. Bayleef
8. Elekid
9. Snubbull
10. Gengar

## NAME THAT POKÉMON I

(pages 10–11)

1. Bayleef
2. Teddiursa
3. Aipom
4. Hoppip
5. Hoothoot
6. Miltank
7. Lapras
8. Psyduck
9. Hitmontop
10. Delibird
11. Sunflora
12. Cyndaquil
13. Crobat
14. Spinarak
15. Wooper
16. Umbreon
17. Unown
18. Stantler
19. Snorlax
20. Bellossom

## POKÉ MATCH I

(pages 12-13)

1. H
2. J
3. N
4. F
5. A
6. D
7. L
8. B
9. K
10. M
11. C
12. O
13. E
14. G
15. I

## POKÉMON STADIUM I
(pages 14–15)
1. Totodile (Water beats Fire)
2. Golem (Rock beats Electric)
3. Magby (Fire beats Grass)
4. Pichu (Electric beats Water)
5. Hoothoot (Flying beats Ground]
6. Smoochum (Psychic beats Ghost)

## EVOLUTION MIX-UP
(pages 16-17)
1. Gyarados
2. Oddish
3. Elekid
4. Ariados
5. Skiploom
6. Charmeleon
7. Bellsprout
8. Cloyster
9. Delibird
10. Hitmonchan

## POKÉMATH
(pages 18–19)
1. 2+1=3
2. 6–3=3
3. 4+2=6
4. 2–0=2
5. 3+1=4
6. 4–2=2
7. 1+0=1
8. 3–3=0
9. 1+1=2
10. 2–1=1
11. 6+0=6
12. 26–6=20

## POKÉ PUZZLE
(pages 20-23)

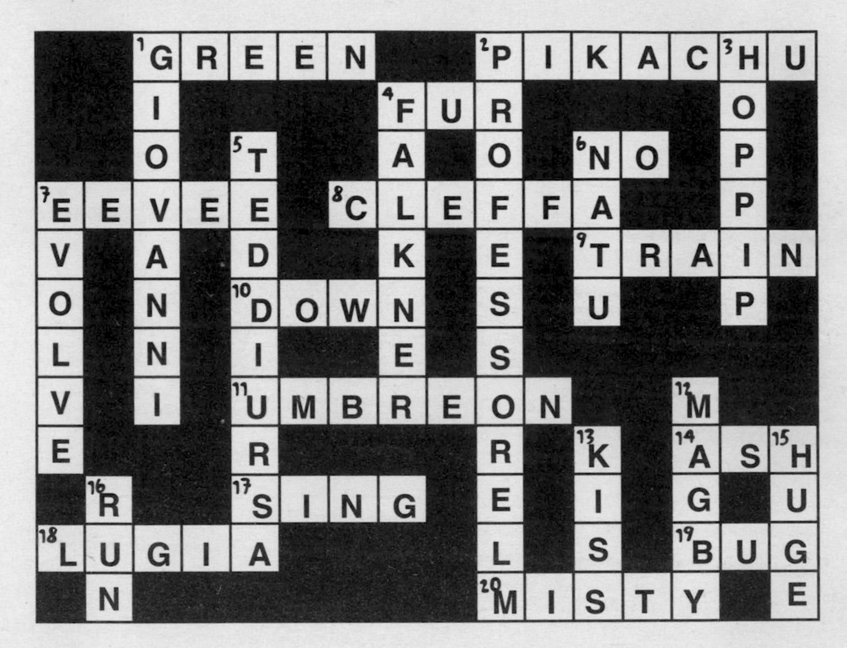


## POKÉ MATCH II
(page 24)
1. B
2. E
3. D
4. F
5. C
6. A

## POKÉ MATCH III
(page 25)
1. C
2. A
3. E
4. B
5. D

## NAME THAT TYPE
(pages 26-27)
1. Fire
2. Water
3. Psychic
4. Fighting
5. Normal
6. Electric
7. Grass
8. Ground

## NAME THAT POKÉMON II
(pages 28-31)
1. C
2. A

3. B
4. B
5. B
6. C
7. B
8. A
9. A
10. C

**COLOR QUIZ**
(pages 32–33)
1. Teddiursa
2. Flaaffy
3. Larvitar
4. Marill
5. Porygon 2
6. Meganium
7. Raichu
8. Corsola
9. Crobat
10. Smoochum

**POKÉMON A–Z**
(pages 34–37)
1. Articuno
2. Bulbasaur
3. Corsola
4. Donphan
5. Espeon
6. Feraligatr
7. Grimer
8. Hypno
9. Igglybuff
10. Jolteon
11. Kingdra
12. Lugia
13. Magikarp
14. Noctowl
15. Octillery
16. Politoed
17. Quilava
18. Remoraid
19. Smeargle
20. Togetic
21. Ursaring
22. Victreebel
23. Wobbuffet
24. Xatu
25. Yanma
26. Zubat

**EPISODE EXPERT II**
(pages 38–41)
1. C
2. B
3. A
4. A
5. C
6. B
7. A
8. A
9. C
10. B

**POKÉMON: UP CLOSE AND PERSONAL II**
(pages 42–43)
1. Hoppip
2. Marill
3. Entei
4. Teddiursa
5. Psyduck
6. Smoochum
7. Houndoom
8. Sunkern
9. Togepi
10. Pineco

## NAME THAT HUMAN
(pages 44–45)
1. Ash
2. Misty
3. Brock
4. Jessie
5. James
6. Hagatha
7. Dr. Wiseman
8. Morty
9. Todd
10. Aya

## TRUE OR FALSE?
(pages 46–49)
1. F
2. T
3. F
4. F
5. T
6. T
7. T
8. F
9. F
10. F
11. F
12. T
13. F
14. F
15. F
16. F
17. T
18. F
19. F
20. F
21. F
22. T
23. T
24. F
25. T

## POKÉMON SUPER SCRAMBLE
(pages 50–51)
1. Sentret
2. Chikorita
3. Ledyba
4. Cleffa
5. Chinchou
6. Sunkern
7. Granbull
8. Suicune
9. Mantine
10. Skarmory

## POKÉ MATCH IV
(pages 52–53)
1. E
2. J
3. G
4. H
5. A
6. K
7. D
8. C
9. B
10. F
11. L
12. I

## NAME THAT POKÉMON III
(pages 54–57)
1. B
2. C
3. A
4. A

5. B
6. B
7. A
8. A
9. A
10. B

**POKÉMON STADIUM II**
(pages 58–59)
1. Yanma (Bug beats Grass)
2. Donphan (Ground beats Poison)
3. Tyrogue (Fighting beats Ice)
4. Delibird (Ice beats Water)
5. Scyther (Bug beats Psychic)
6. Quilava (Fire beats Bug)
7. Elekid (Electric beats Flying)
8. Croconaw (Water beats Ground)

**TEAM ROCKET TRIVIA**
(pages 60–63)
1. bottle caps
2. Butch and Cassidy
3. nurse
4. Wobbuffet
5. Sunflora
6. Shuckle
7. Arbotank
8. Lickitung
9. money
10. Meowth
11. mask
12. Poison
13. net
14. language
15. robot

**EPISODE EXPERT III**
(pages 64–67)
1. B
2. A
3. C
4. B
5. A
6. B
7. C
8. A
9. B
10. B

# Scoring Chart

Are you a Johto Genius? To find out, count up the number of questions you got right. There were nearly 300 questions in all. The more questions you answered correctly, the more you score.

**1–50 = Stuck in Pallet Town**
You are kind of like Ash when he was just starting out. It will take a lot of study and practice before you are on the road to becoming a Pokémon Master. But if Ash can do it, so can you!

**51–100 = On the Road**
You are doing pretty well on your Pokémon journey, but you still have a way to go. Keep practicing!

**101–150 = Badge of Honor**
You've got what it takes to win gym badges, but you need to broaden your horizons and study Pokémon all over the world.

**151–200 = Winner Takes All**
Congratulations! You've got what it takes to win all kinds of Pokémon competitions. Keep up the good work.

**OVER 200 = Johto Genius**
You are legendary for your knowledge of Pokémon. Other trainers look up to you. Don't let them down!